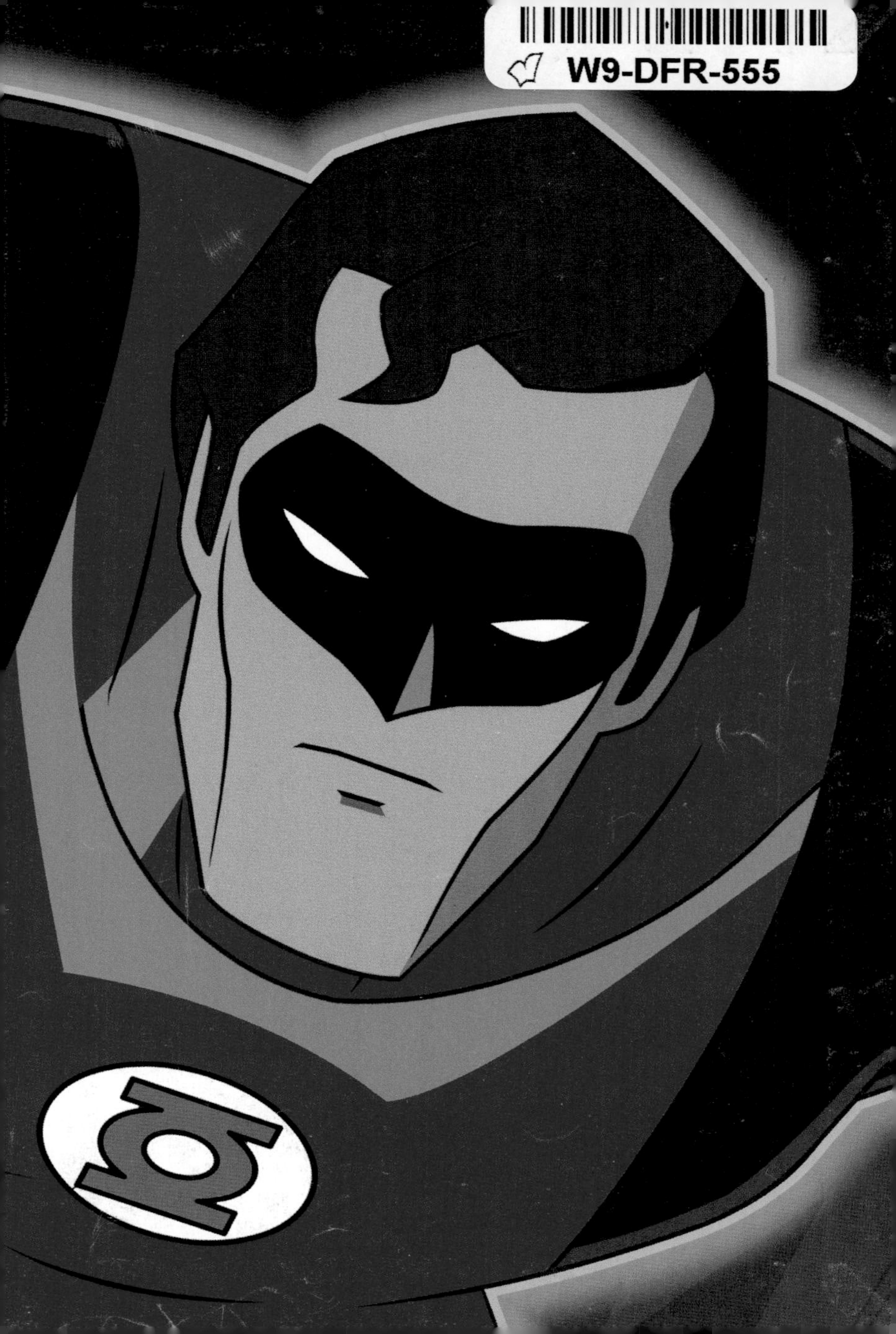

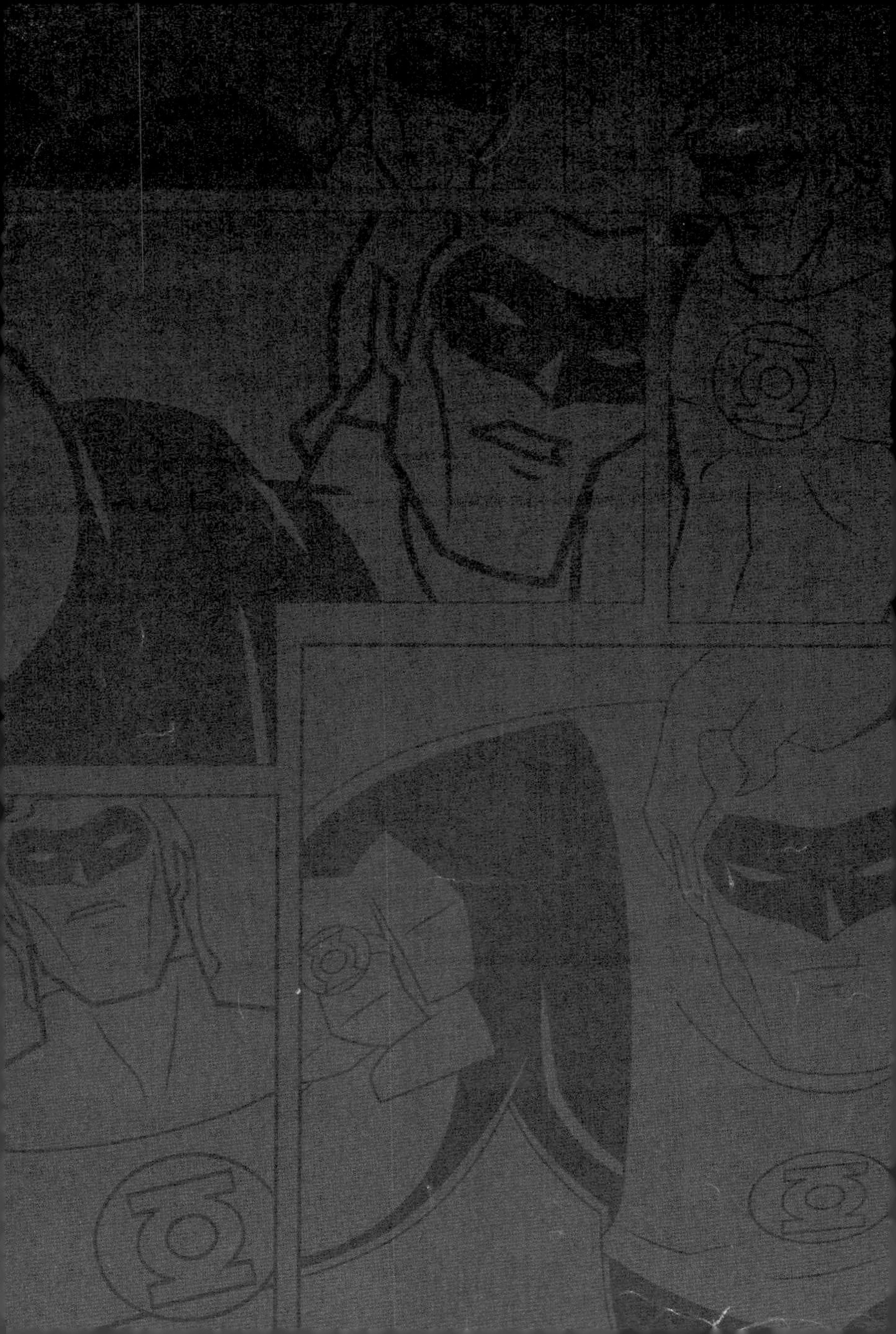

AS THE NEWEST MEMBER OF AN INTERGALACTIC PEACEKEEPING FORCE KNOWN AS THE GREEN LANTERN CORPS, HAL JORDAN FIGHTS EVIL AND PROUDLY WEARS THE UNIFORM AND RING OF . . .

SUPER DC HEROES™

GREEN LANTERN™

BATTLE OF THE BLUE LANTERNS

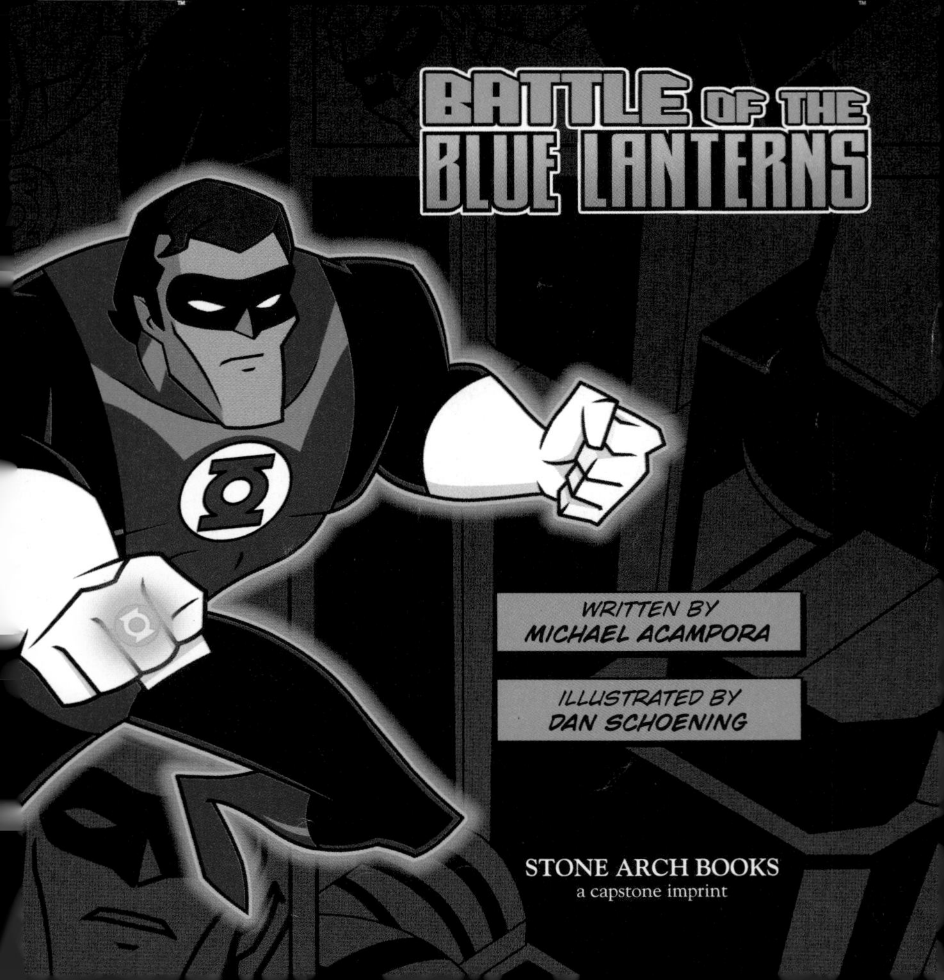

WRITTEN BY
MICHAEL ACAMPORA

ILLUSTRATED BY
DAN SCHOENING

STONE ARCH BOOKS
a capstone imprint

Published by Stone Arch Books in 2011
A Capstone Imprint
151 Good Counsel Drive, P.O. Box 669
Mankato, Minnesota 56002
www.capstonepub.com

Library of Congress Cataloging-in-Publication Data

Acampora, Michael Vincent, 1989-
  Battle of the Blue Lanterns / written by Michael Vincent Acampora ;
illustrated by Dan Schoening.
    p. cm. -- (DC super heroes. Green Lantern)
  ISBN 978-1-4342-2608-2 (library binding) -- ISBN 978-1-4342-3085-0 (pbk.)
  1. Graphic novels. [1. Graphic novels. 2. Superheroes--Fiction. 3. Youths'
writings.] I. Schoening, Dan, ill. II. Title.
  PZ7.7.A28Bat 2011
  741.5'973--dc22   2010025597

Summary: In the far reaches of space, deadly Manhunter robots attack a small
planet and its people. Luckily, Hal Jordan, a member of the Green Lantern
Corps is close by! The super hero stops the first wave of mechanical killers,
but hundreds more quickly follow. Soon, Hal is overwhelmed, unable to hold
off the assault any longer. Then suddenly, two members of the Blue Lantern
Corps restore his energy. Hal is thankful for the help, but it comes with a price.
They want Hal to give up his green ring and join the Blue Lanterns . . . or
suffer the consequences.

Art Director: Bob Lentz
Designer: Hilary Wacholz
Production Specialist: Michelle Biedscheid

Printed in the United States of America in Stevens Point, Wisconsin.
092010
005934WZS11

TABLE OF CONTENTS

CHAPTER 1

VACATION'S OVER!

Green Lantern Hal Jordan leaned back and smiled. Today was the first time since joining the Green Lantern Corps that he hoped to take the day off. With no missions to save the universe on his schedule, Hal flew to a beach on the beautiful planet Orios. With his ring, the super hero constructed a big green hammock. He lay looking out at the ocean, watching many alien animals he had never seen before.

WHODOOSH! A giant, scaly creature jumped out of the water.

At first, Hal thought it was a dolphin, but as he looked closer, the strange orange fish appeared more like a horse. At that same moment, three purple birds flew overhead. **CRUNCH! CRUNCH!** The strange creature opened its jaws, swallowed up the birds, and splashed back down in the water.

Hal was not surprised. Ever since he had become a Green Lantern and traveled around the universe, the super hero had seen all sorts of animals. Most of them looked very different from those on Earth.

After watching the creatures for a moment, Hal lay back in his hammock. He closed his eyes and decided to take a much needed nap.

BEEP! Suddenly, Hal's Green Lantern ring demanded his attention.

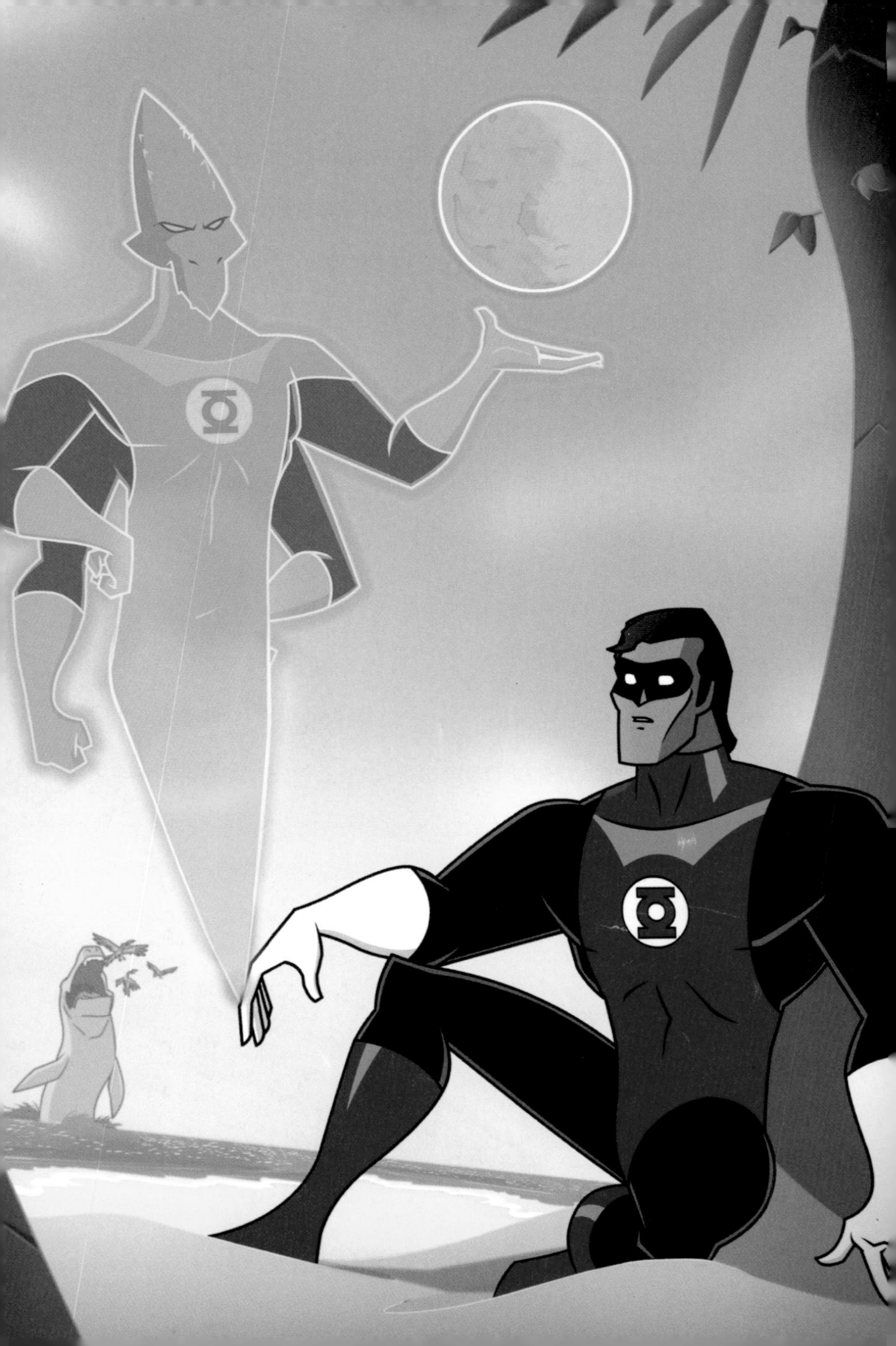

A green hologram of an alien with four arms popped out of it. Hal's hammock disappeared. He fell down onto the sand.

THUD!

It's Salaak, Hal thought. *Must be time for a new mission.*

"Hal Jordan, your rest is over," the image of Salaak said.

"I had a feeling," Hal with a smile, "but I didn't even get to catch up on sleep."

"You need to report to the planet Nokyo One," the alien continued. "I've received reports of Manhunter robots attacking a human city there, and you are the closest Green Lantern. I have sent the directions to the planet to your ring. Travel to Nokyo One and protect the city. Good luck, Hal." The hologram of Salaak disappeared.

Manhunters? thought Hal. Manhunters were a race of androids the Guardians of the Universe had created before they formed the Green Lantern Corps. The androids were built to maintain peace, but had become corrupted and very dangerous.

"Time to save the universe again," he said to himself. With that, he raised his fist into the sky and took off through space.

* * *

When Hal arrived on Nokyo One, he immediately saw the Manhunter robots as he flew toward the city. *That's strange,* Hal thought. *There aren't enough robots to take over a planet. What are they doing here?*

As he reached the surface of the planet, Hal willed his ring to construct two boxing gloves.

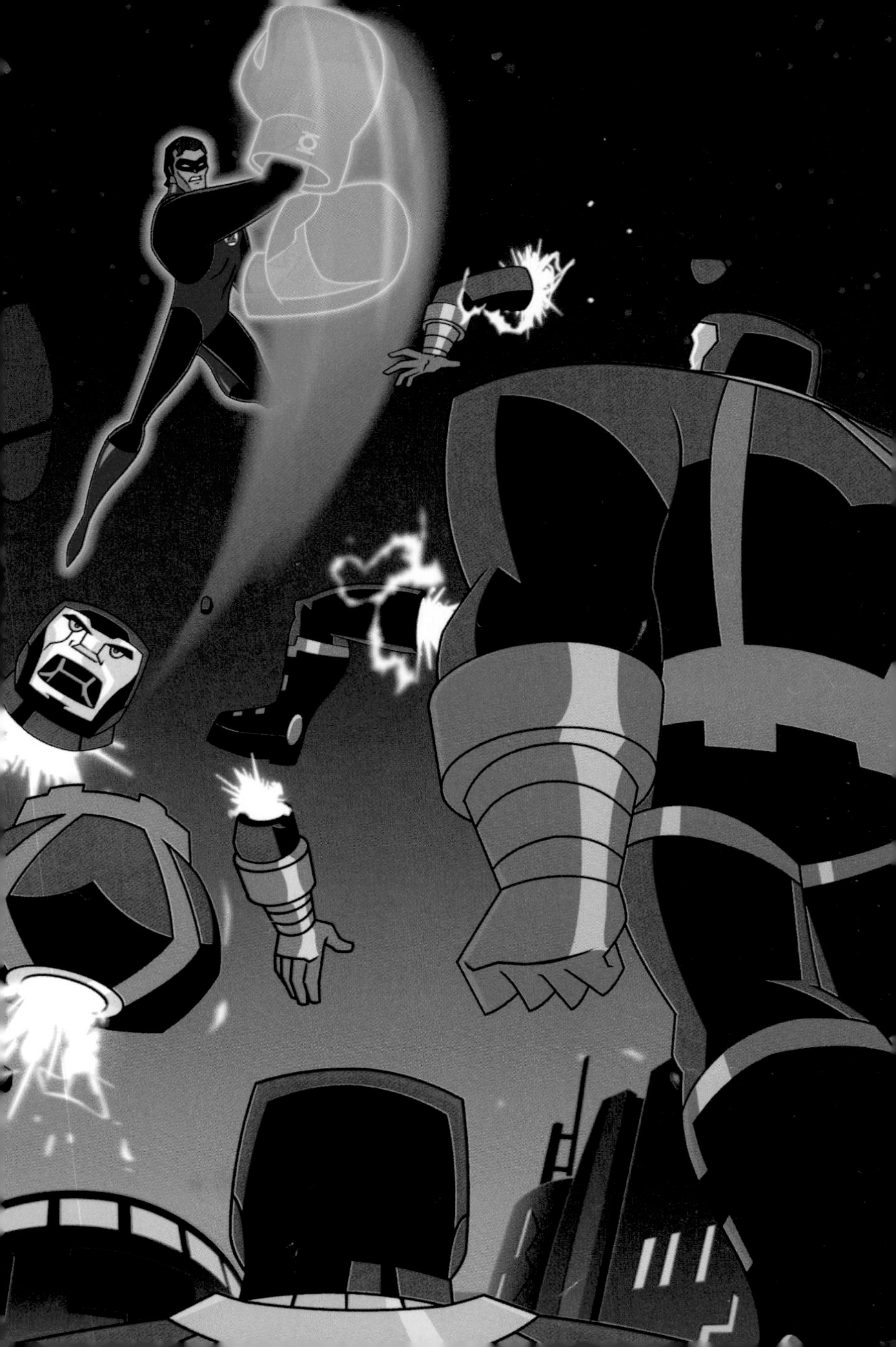

Hal placed the superpowered gloves on each hand and flew directly at a group of the Manhunters.

"In this corner, a broken robot!" Hal shouted. **Ka-Paннnnng!** He punched a Manhunter as hard as he could. A thousand tiny pieces flew through the air.

Hal didn't have time to celebrate. Another Manhunter robot was flying straight at him. "Batter up!" he yelled, transforming his boxing gloves into a green baseball bat.

KRAK! He swung the bat at the charging Manhunter and destroyed it. The people who had gathered on the streets to watch the Green Lantern save their city began to cheer. Suddenly, Hal heard a woman scream. "Help!" the woman cried. "That building is burning! Save us!"

Hal looked around. Out of the corner of his eye, he spotted a large apartment building. It had caught fire during his battle with the Manhunters. He thought quickly, deciding the best way to put out the blaze. Then the super hero spotted a large river a few hundred feet away.

With his ring, the super hero made a fire hose and pointed it at the river. It quickly filled with water. Then Hal pointed the hose at the building and unleashed the water.

Splash! Within seconds, the building had stopped burning.

The people trapped inside came running out onto the street, relieved and grateful.

"Thank you!" a woman said to Hal.

"No problem," Hal replied. "Just doing my job —"

"Look out behind you!" another person interrupted.

Hal turned around just in time to see ten more Manhunter robots flying at him.

"That's enough!" Hal said. He pointed his ring at the robots and created a giant bubble around them. They were trapped. Hal flung the bubble into space, sending the robots far away, where he hoped they would never be trouble again.

"Another planet saved!" Hal said.

Then suddenly, Hal's ring cried out, "WARNING! Incoming enemies!"

Hal looked up at the sky. Hundreds more robots were heading straight toward the city! "Maybe I spoke too soon," the super hero said.

CHAPTER 2

ATTACK OF THE MANHUNTERS!

I've never fought this many enemies at once! Hal thought as he flew toward the incoming robots. The Green Lantern needed a weapon to fight with. Using his ring, Hal created a giant green sword. As soon as he was close to the attackers, he swung the sword as hard as he could at the robots.

CLANK! The first five Manhunters exploded on impact.

"Power levels at 50 percent," said Hal's green ring.

Through the smoke of the destroyed robots, Hal could see hundreds more coming toward him. He gulped. *I need to do better than that!* he thought.

Hal focused hard, attempting to create another giant sword with his ring. But the weapon didn't appear.

"Power levels at 10 percent," said his ring.

Hal weakened as well. *I've got to keep fighting!* he thought.

The Green Lantern flew toward the nearest robot and fired a beam of energy from his ring. The robot dodged it and blasted Hal with its own laser beam.

"Power levels at 1 percent," said Hal's ring. The super hero's eyes began to close, and he was about to pass out.

Suddenly, Hal felt power growing within.

"Power levels at 30 percent," exclaimed Hal's ring.

Huh?! the Green Lantern thought.

"Power levels at 100 percent," said the ring.

What's going on?! Hal felt all of his strength flowing back and prepared to attack the robots again.

"Power levels at 200 percent," Hal's ring said.

"Two-hundred percent?!" Hal shouted.

"Do not worry, Green Lantern Hal Jordan," said a calm voice. "All is well."

Hal didn't have time to look for the source of the voice. The Manhunter robots were about to reach the planet's surface.

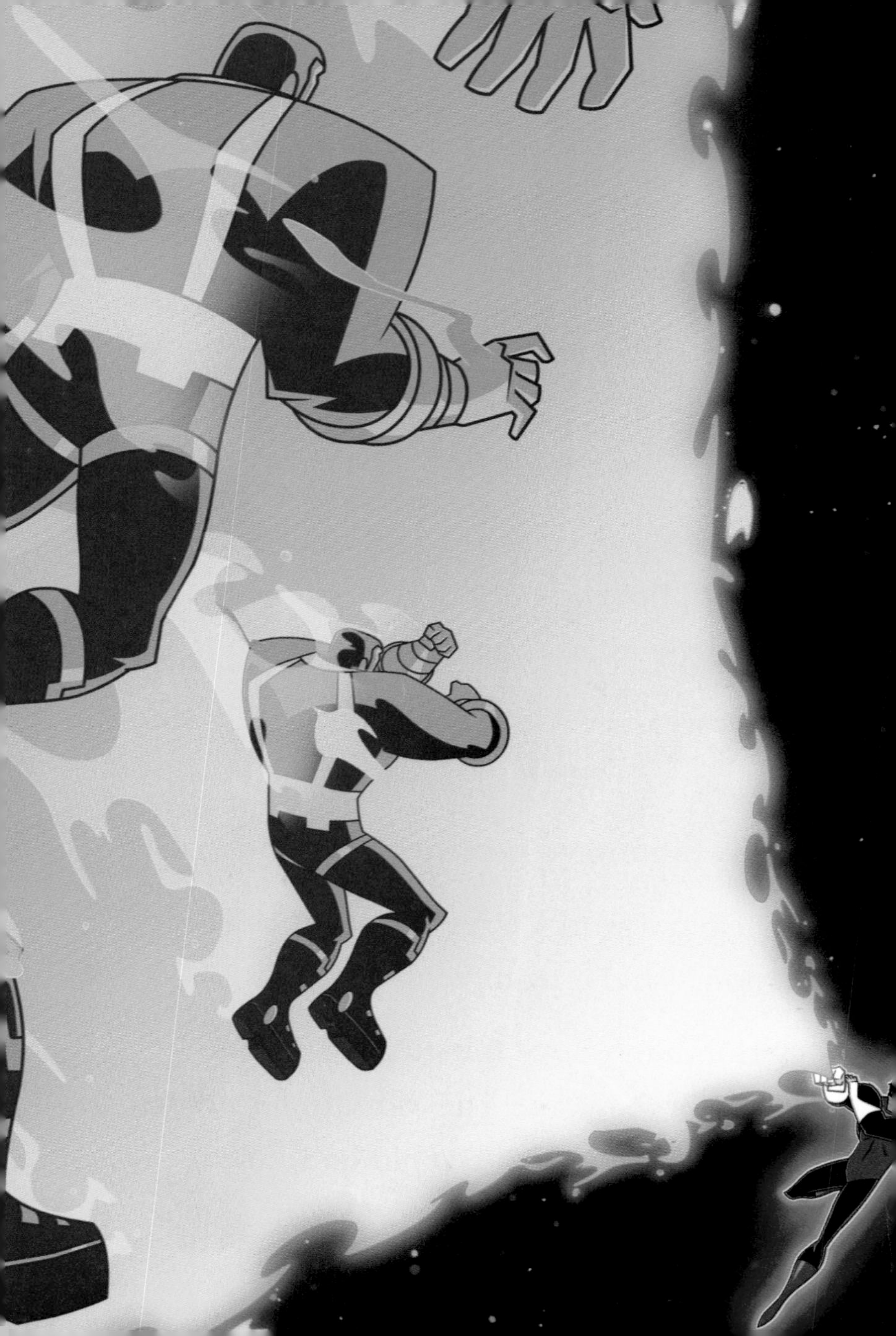

Hal focused again. This time, he felt a massive amount of energy flow through him. He channeled the energy into a giant green blast and shot it at the Manhunters.

KA-BOOM! The blast was larger than any Hal had ever created. It destroyed nearly every robot. Only a handful had escaped. They quickly retreated into space.

"Got 'em!" exclaimed Hal.

The calm voice spoke again. "Excellent work, Hal Jordan."

Hal spun around. Floating behind him was an alien with white skin, no nose, and a long tentacle at the back of his head. The alien wore a uniform like Hal's — except it was blue. "It is I, Saint Walker," said the alien, "and this is Brother Sepdifer." He pointed to a figure beside him.

Hal had encountered Saint Walker in previous adventures, but he'd never met Brother Sepdifer. "Thanks for the help, Walker," Hal said. He pointed at Brother Sepdifer. "Is he a Blue Lantern, too?"

"Correct, Hal Jordan," said Saint Walker. "We are both Blue Lanterns."

"Were you the ones who super-charged my ring?" asked Hal.

"Yes. We are fueled by the power of hope," explained Saint Walker. "We channeled all of the hope from the citizens of Nokyo One into your ring. The power of hope became your strength."

"Thank you for the help," said Hal.

"You are welcome, Hal Jordan," said Saint Walker. Brother Sepdifer stood silently, nodding his head with approval.

"Why doesn't he talk?" asked Hal.

"Brother Sepdifer has pledged a vow of silence. He is currently spending one year without speaking to show his dedication to the Blue Lantern Corps and to the power of hope," replied Saint Walker.

Hal grinned. "You guys are crazy," said the super hero with a smile.

"We are not crazy, Hal Jordan," said Saint Walker, "but we must ask you to come with us."

"Come with you where?" questioned Hal.

"You must travel with us to the Blue Lantern home planet of Odym," said Saint Walker. "You will train to become a Blue Lantern and join our quest to spread hope throughout the universe."

Hal began to laugh. "You guys really are crazy! I'm not coming with you anywhere! I'm a Green Lantern. I'm powered by my will!" shouted Hal. "And right now, my will is to go after the rest of those Manhunters!"

"I am sorry, Hal Jordan," said Saint Walker, "but your mission must wait. It is most important that you come with us to Odym *now*. There is no time to waste."

"Look, I appreciate your help earlier," repeated Hal. "But I have to follow those robots and make sure they never return. *That* is what's most important." To show off his power, Hal created a green fighter jet.

"You must learn about the power of hope!" shouted Saint Walker. Even though he had raised his voice, it was still very calm and peaceful. He spoke to Hal as if he were already his close friend.

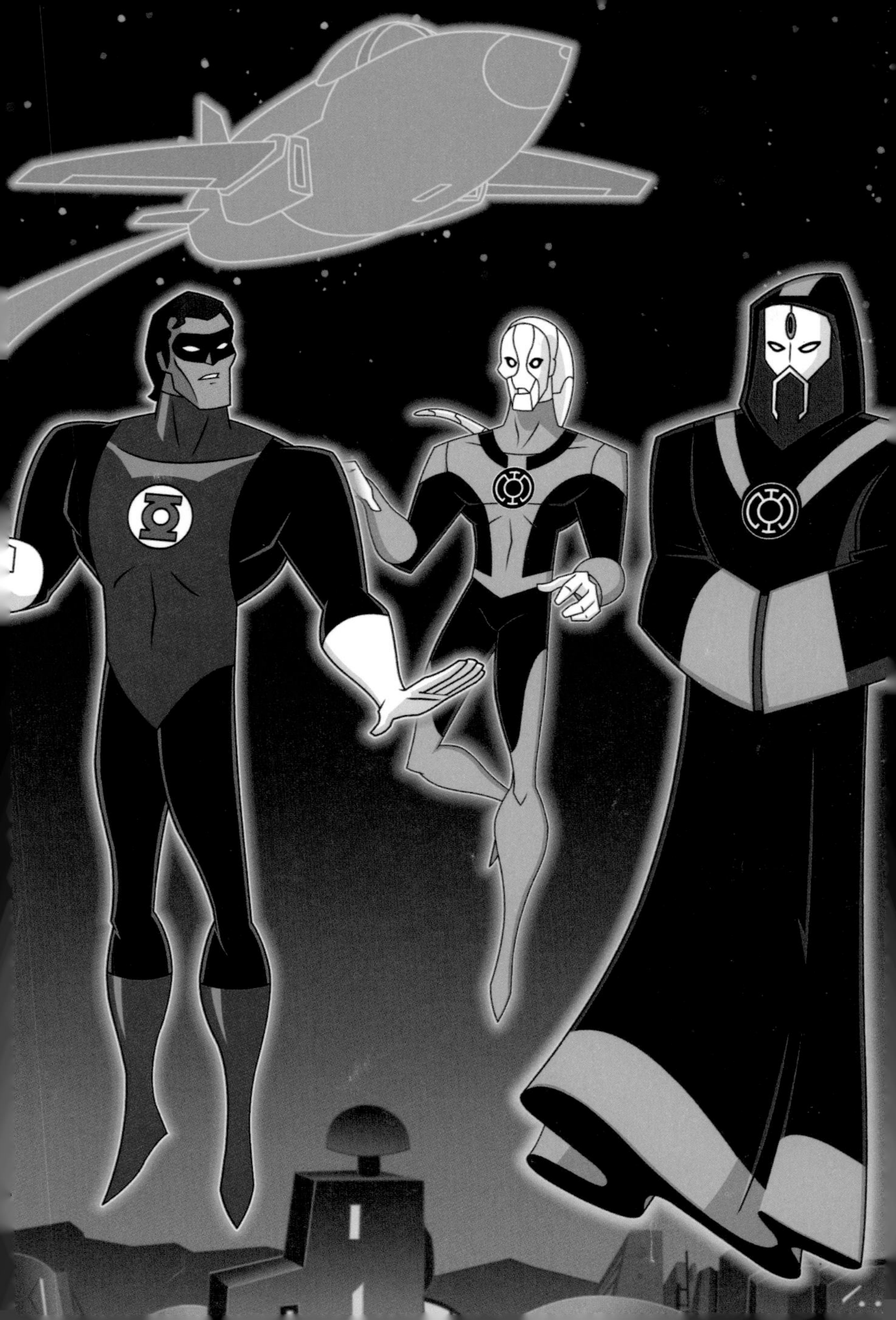

"I'm sorry, guys, but hope alone isn't enough to save the universe," said Hal. "The only way I can make a difference is by using my willpower to get things done. Thanks again for your offer, but I'm going to stop the Manhunters now."

Hal jumped into the cockpit of the jet and blasted off for space. He left the Blue Lanterns behind.

ZWWWOOOMMMM!

Saint Walker turned to Brother Sepdifer. "Hal Jordan is not yet aware of the bond between hope and willpower," he said to his silent comrade.

Brother Sepdifer shook his head. The two Blue Lanterns watched as Hal's jet flew toward the stars.

CHAPTER 3

VOYAGE TO KIRDON

As he left Nokyo One's atmosphere, Hal spoke to his ring. "Can you trace the fuel trails that the fleeing robots left behind?" asked Hal.

"One moment," chimed the ring.

A few seconds later, Hal's ring had the answer. "Locked on to Manhunter robot fuel trails. They lead to the planet Kirdon, which is approximately 7.63 million miles from our present location."

"We'd better hurry up then," said Hal.

"Affirmative. Focusing all power on acceleration," replied his ring. The green jet sped up, and Hal was flying faster than he ever had before.

*   *   *

After several hours, Hal could see the planet Kirdon from the cockpit of his green jet. The planet was a bright orange orb. It looked like a giant fireball.

"Ring, are you sure this isn't a star?" asked Hal.

"Correct. This is not a star. It is the planet Kirdon," answered the ring.

If you say so, thought Hal. *It doesn't look like any planet I've ever seen, though.*

As Hal flew closer toward the planet, his ring alerted him again.

BEEP! BEEP! BEEP! BEEP!

"WARNING!" said the ring. "Kirdon's temperatures are incredibly high! Keep your shield up at all times while on the surface."

"Good to know," Hal said.

He streaked toward the planet. Nearing the surface, the Green Lantern noticed that Kirdon didn't just *look* like it was on fire — it was covered with flames! Smoke and molten lava blanketed the planet's entire landscape.

How could a Manhunter base be here?! Hal wondered. *Nothing could survive in this environment.*

Hal continued to fly over the fires. He looked for a place to land. After a few minutes, he spotted a large rock sticking up out of the sea of lava. He landed his jet on the rock and jumped out.

"Shields at 100 percent," said his ring.

"Thanks," said Hal. "Can you find the actual location of the Manhunter base?"

"The base is eighteen miles north of our present location," replied the ring.

"Let's go!" said Hal. He jumped in the air and began flying north toward the robots' headquarters. His ring kept a shield around him to protect him from the heat.

After flying north for a few moments, Hal dodged a giant pillar of fire that shot up into the air. *WHOOOOSH!* It nearly knocked Hal out of the sky.

"WARNING! Shields at 80 percent!" exclaimed Hal's ring.

I need to be more careful, thought Hal, tumbling toward the sea of lava beneath him. He quickly recovered in midair.

"Approaching Manhunter base," warned Hal's ring. "Proceed with extreme caution."

"What are you talking about?" asked Hal. "I don't see anything that looks like a base. All I see is fire!"

Hal stopped flying and floated above the fires. He looked in every direction for signs of the Manhunter headquarters.

"Aha!" Hal finally exclaimed. Out of the corner of his eye, Hal spotted a small mountain peak sticking out of the flames. It looked like a volcano that had sunk into the sea of lava.

An underground base, Hal realized. *That's got to be it.* He flew over to the mountain peak and hovered high above it.

"Multiple Manhunter signals detected below," said his ring.

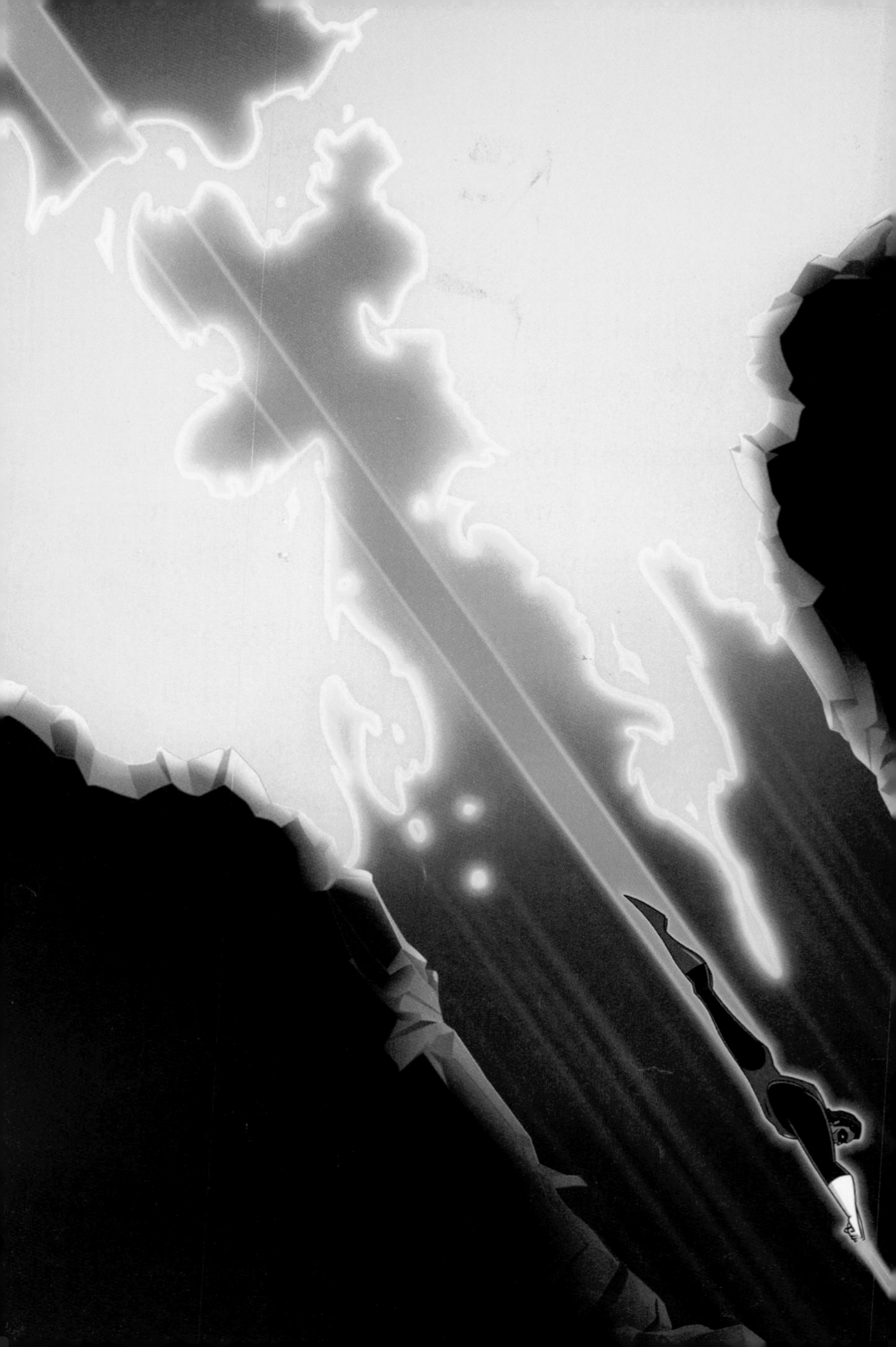

The Green Lantern flew down toward the mountain. On the peak, a huge crater seemed to lead to the inside of the base.

"We're going in!" yelled Hal with a grin. **THUDOOOMMMMMM!!** The Green Lantern dived down into the giant hole, flying at full speed. The crater led to a long dark tunnel within the mountain. He sped through the corridor, the bright green light of his ring guiding the way.

Hal began to think that his ring had made a mistake and that this was not the Manhunters' base after all. He was about to turn around when his ring finally spoke.

"Approaching a large chamber," said the ring. "Use caution."

Finally! thought Hal. *This has got to be their headquarters.*

Suddenly, Hal could see a light at the end of the tunnel. He flew toward it and into a massive stone room. The super hero realized he had reached the center of the mountain. Glancing around, he quickly determined that this was not just a hollowed-out mountain. Hundreds of high-tech machines filled the room. Some were repairing broken robots. Others looked like they were creating new ones. Hundreds of Manhunters hung on the walls, plugged in and charging like oversized computers.

This is definitely their base, thought Hal. *Now I just need to figure out how to destroy it!*

Hal didn't have time to think. **THUD!** Something smacked the back of his head, knocking him to the ground.

"Welcome, human," said a booming, robotic voice. "Prepare for elimination!"

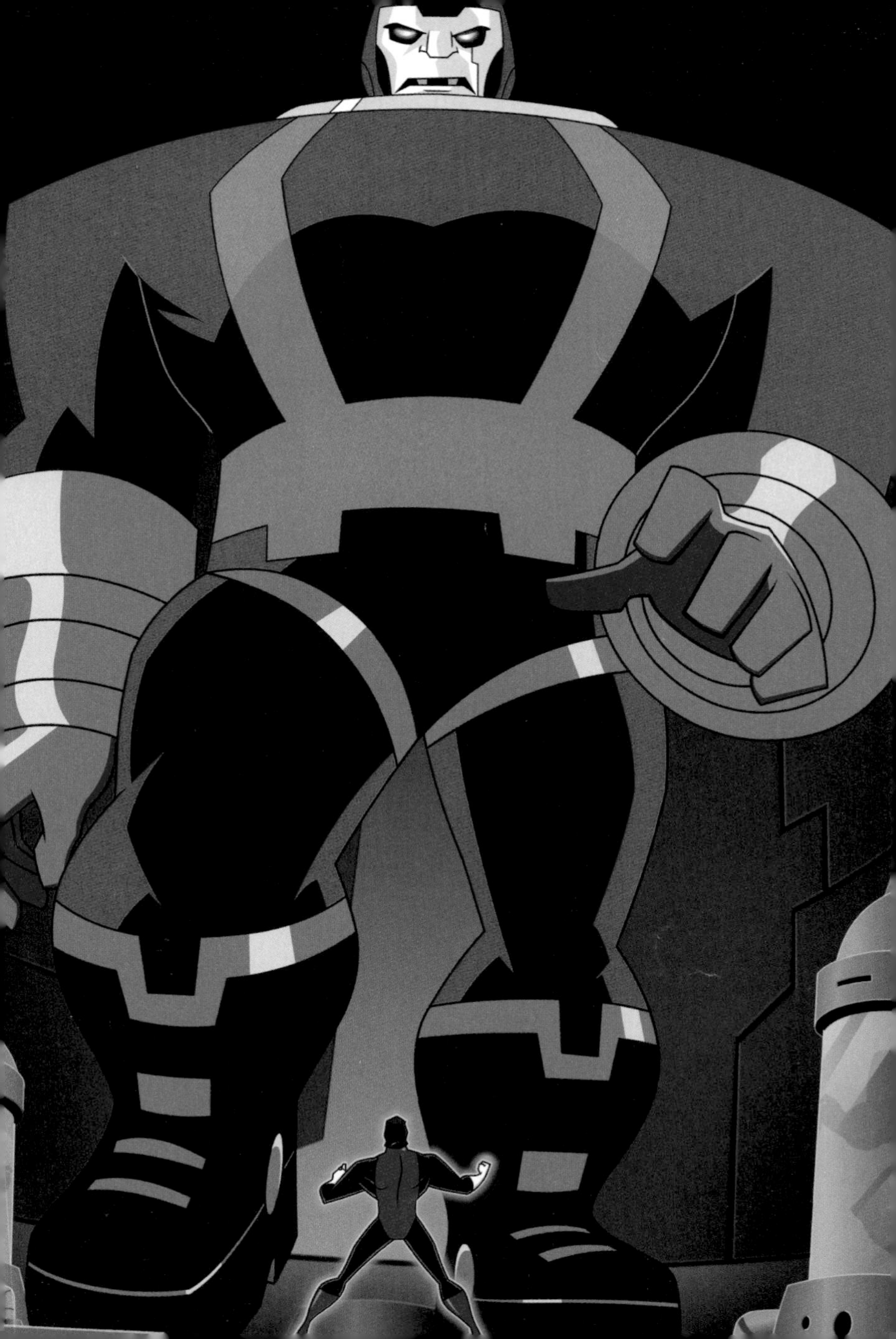

CHAPTER 4

ENTER THE GRANDMASTER

Hal looked up from his position on the ground. Towering over him was a robot unlike any that he had ever seen before. It was more than a hundred feet tall and fifty feet wide. The giant machine resembled a Manhunter, but something about it was different. Hal looked closer at his attacker. Not only did it resemble a Manhunter, it was made up of thousands of Manhunters!

Hal realized that he might be in trouble.

"Shields at 70 percent," his ring warned him.

Hal climbed to his feet and faced his opponent. "You must be the one behind the attacks on Nokyo One!" he shouted.

"Correct, human," answered the colossal robot. "I am the Grandmaster. The Manhunter army is under my command."

"You attacked innocent people! Why?!" asked Hal.

"Our planet is dying," Grandmaster said. "The core is erupting, and the entire surface is covered in flames. It will not be long before Kirdon explodes."

"But why attack Nokyo One?" asked Hal. The super hero was growing impatient.

"Nokyo One is the closest suitable planet for our needs. We plan to eliminate the human population there and colonize the planet," said the Grandmaster.

"Sorry," said Hal, raising his ring out in front of him, "but I can't let you do that."

Hal created a giant green lasso and spun it around in the air. WHOOOOSH!

He tossed it at the Grandmaster, catching the massive robot around its left leg. Hal tugged on the lasso, attempting to pull the Grandmaster to the ground.

The Grandmaster did not move an inch. Instead, it ripped the green lasso off of its leg. "Eliminate him!" it screamed.

Hearing their master's command, hundreds of smaller Manhunters detached themselves from the walls and flew directly at Hal. "NO MAN ESCAPES THE MANHUNTERS!" they all yelled in menacing robotic voices.

Stay sharp, Hal told himself.

Hal created a huge pair of green shears with his ring. He used it to chop two of the closest robots in half. Then he changed the shears into a hammer, and swung it at the next closest robots. **THUD!** Hal destroyed five more Manhunters. Then, Hal realized that these basic tools would not be enough to take out the entire army.

I need some backup, he thought.

Hal thought of his fellow Green Lanterns back on the planet Oa. He focused all of his willpower into his ring and tried to make the strongest constructs he could. Out of his ring emerged several green holographic versions of his Green Lantern friends, including Kilowog, Arisia, and Salaak!

The constructs of the Corps members flew at the attacking Manhunter robots, firing energy beams at them.

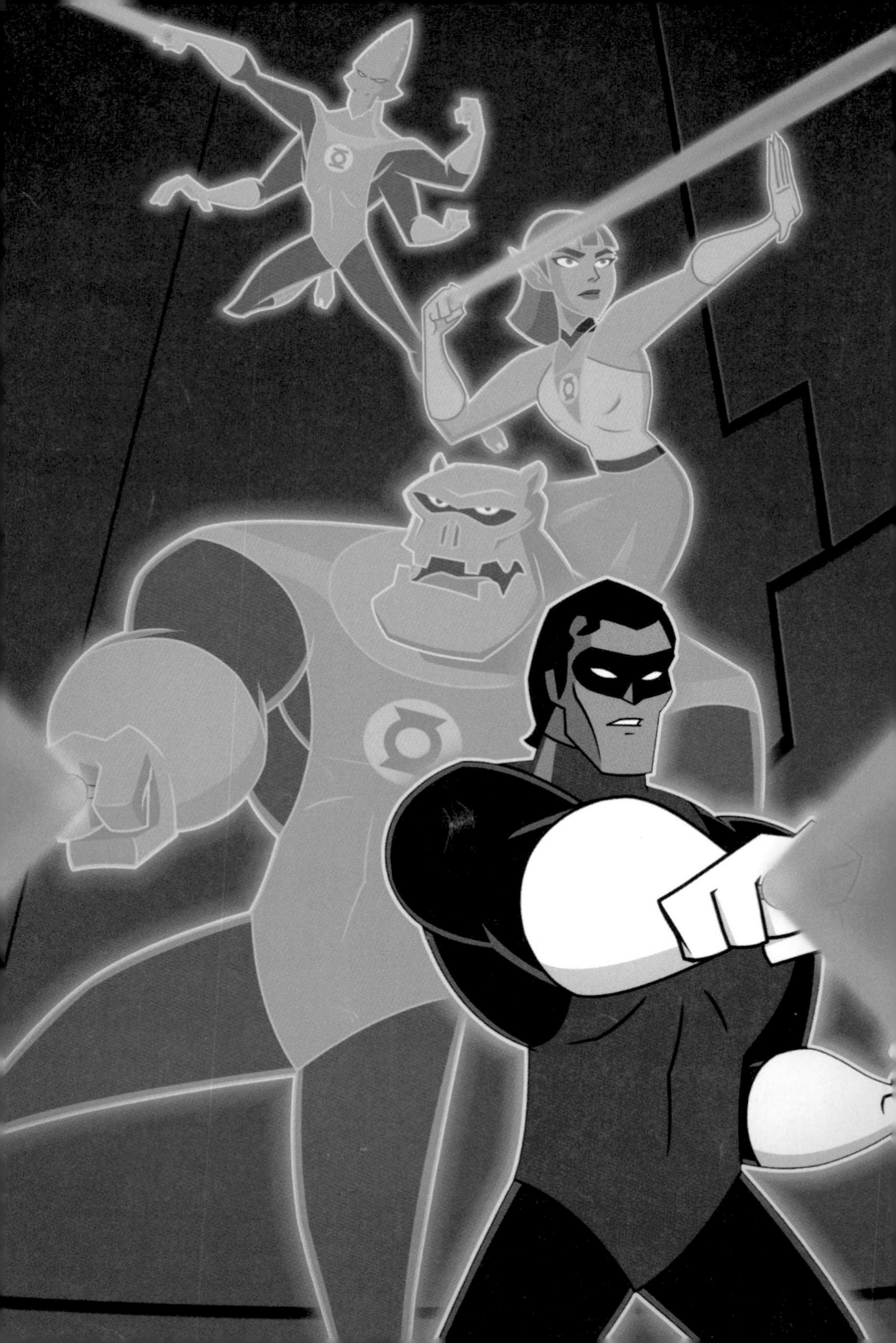

They were able to destroy almost fifty robots, but Hal was only strong enough to maintain the constructs for a few seconds before they disappeared.

"WARNING!" chimed his ring. "Power levels at 15 percent."

"I only have one more chance," Hal said. "I need to focus all of my will."

Another swarm of Manhunters zoomed toward Hal. "Time for some target practice!" shouted Hal.

He shot a dozen green energy beams at the attacking robots. Most of the energy beams hit the Manhunters in the middle of their helmets, causing them to explode. Other energy beams were so powerful that they were able to destroy two robots at once.

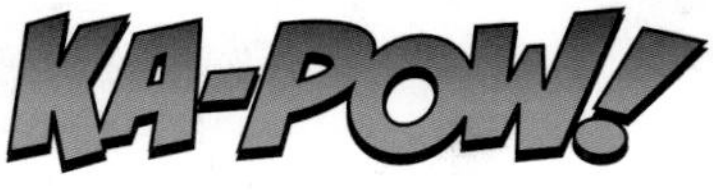
KA-POW!

More Manhunters quickly approached Hal from the side, and he fired another series of energy beams at them. One energy beam tore straight through a Manhunter, hitting the wall of the mountain and creating a giant hole.

WHOOOOSH! Lava suddenly rushed into the chamber through the hole in the side of the mountain.

"WARNING! WARNING!" said Hal's ring. "Temperatures in this chamber will soon reach critical levels. Evacuation is highly recommended."

"I guess I figured out how I'm going to destroy the base!" Hal shouted with a grin.

ZZRRRRTT! From out of nowhere, the Grandmaster knocked Hal to the ground with a laser blast.

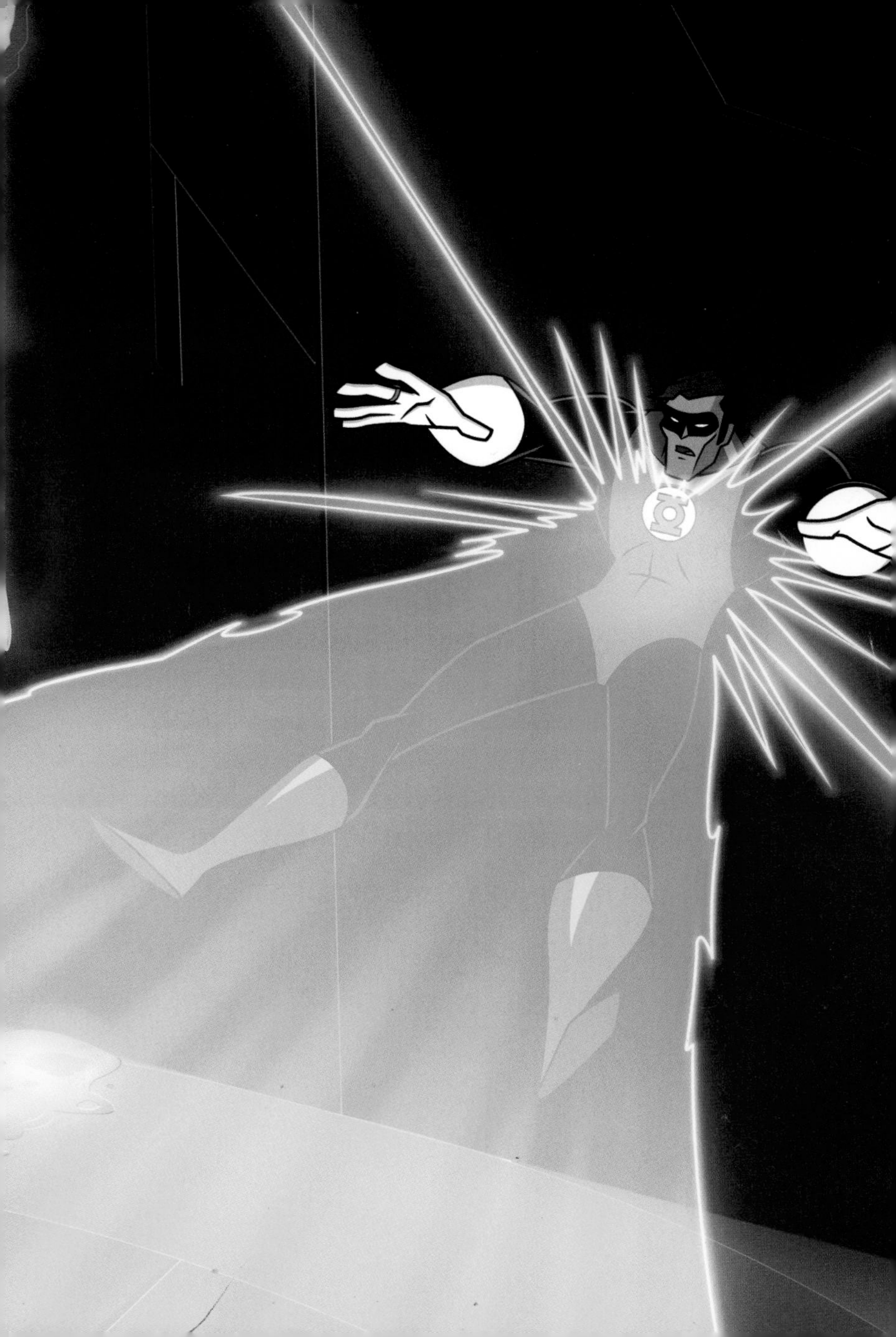

"Power levels at 4 percent," warned Hal's ring.

A Manhunter landed on the ground next to Hal, and placed its foot on Hal's neck. "NO MAN ESCAPES THE MANHUNTERS!" the robot yelled.

I'm doomed, Hal thought.

ZZAPPPPPPP! Then suddenly, a blue energy beam blasted through the Manhunter's chest and destroyed it.

Hal was saved!

From behind Hal, Saint Walker, the Blue Lantern, stepped out of the shadows. Brother Sepdifer was again floating beside him. "As I told you before, Hal Jordan," Saint Walker said, "you must never give up hope!"

CHAPTER 5

RETURN OF THE BLUE LANTERNS

Hal could already feel the power flowing back into him, which he now knew was a result of the Blue Lanterns' presence.

"I didn't realize that you guys could fire energy beams or make constructs," Hal said to the Blue Lanterns. "I thought you were just living, breathing power-chargers."

"Our rings possess many of the same abilities as yours," answered Saint Walker, "but with an important restriction."

"What's that?" asked Hal.

"Our rings only work when in the presence of a Green Lantern. Hope is useless without the willpower to act upon it, Hal Jordan," explained Saint Walker.

"Well then it's a good thing I'm here to rescue you guys!" Hal joked. "Now, let's get rid of this Grandmaster — *and* his army!"

Hal, Saint Walker, and Brother Sepdifer fired energy beams in every direction.

Within seconds, they had destroyed nearly every Manhunter in the chamber. The remaining robots flew toward the Grandmaster and attached themselves to his casing.

The massive machine was now even larger and more powerful than before.

"Lanterns!" the machine bellowed. "I will extinguish your light forever!"

"Not going to happen!" yelled Hal.

Hal nodded at the Blue Lanterns. All three created constructs of giant superpowered chains. Hal wrapped his chains around the Grandmaster's legs, while the Blue Lanterns chained together the Grandmaster's arms.

"Take him down!" shouted Hal.

On his command, each Lantern pulled hard on their chains. The Grandmaster began to teeter. Hal tensed his muscles and pulled as hard as he could. The Grandmaster fell to the ground of the chamber — and into the molten lava!

The lava immediately started melting the Grandmaster's armor.

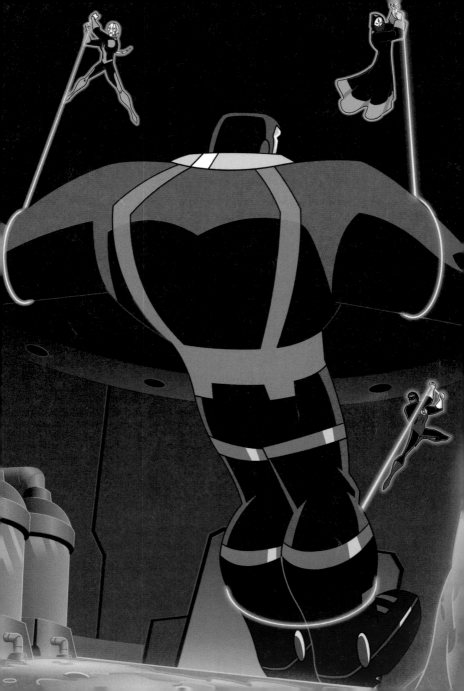

Hal's ring sounded an alert. "WARNING! The Grandmaster is about to explode, which will destroy this entire mountain. Evacuate immediately!"

"You heard the ring!" yelled Hal to the Blue Lanterns. "Let's get out of here!"

The three Lanterns rocketed through the tunnel opening, racing toward the surface.

KA-BOOM! The Lanterns heard a loud explosion beneath them. "That must have been the Grandmaster," said Saint Walker. "Good riddance."

Suddenly, fire shot up through the tunnel. **FWOOOSHHHHHH!** The three Lanterns flew at super-speed, barely escaping the tunnel before it was fully consumed in fire. As they reached the surface, the entire mountain crumbled into the sea of lava.

Hal and the Blue Lanterns watched in awe as the planet collapsed in on itself.

Saint Walker turned to face the Green Lantern. "Hal Jordan, we followed you to this planet in order to bring you back to Odym with us," said Walker. "But we see now that we cannot simply have you join our ranks as a Blue Lantern."

Walker smiled at Hal. "The fusion of hope and will is the most powerful force in existence," he said. "If the universe is to be protected, it must include both Green *and* Blue Lanterns."

"I couldn't have said it better myself," replied Hal.

"I am glad that you agree," said Saint Walker. Despite the danger they had just faced, his voice was completely calm.

"So . . . can your rings do any other tricks?" asked Hal.

"We know no tricks," explained Saint Walker. "But our rings do possess another ability in addition to those of your ring."

"Oh? What's that?" asked Hal, curious.

"We can create a construct of a person's most hopeful future," revealed Saint Walker.

"Can you show me mine?" said Hal.

Saint Walker closed his eyes. He placed one hand on Hal's shoulder and put his other hand out in front of him.

All of a sudden, a blue construct of a man appeared before them. He resembled Hal, but appeared slightly older. He was wearing a Green Lantern uniform similar to Hal's.

The hologram looked very regal, almost as if he were a king.

"Who . . . who is this?" asked Hal.

"This is you, Hal Jordan," answered Saint Walker. "This is who the universe hopes you will become — the greatest Green Lantern of all."

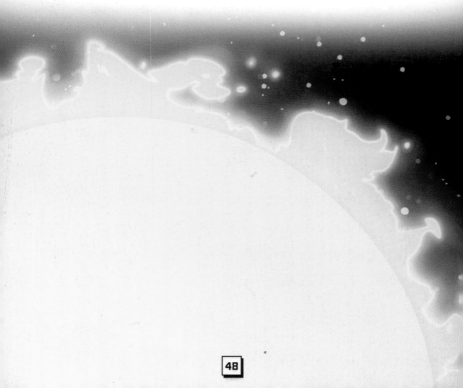

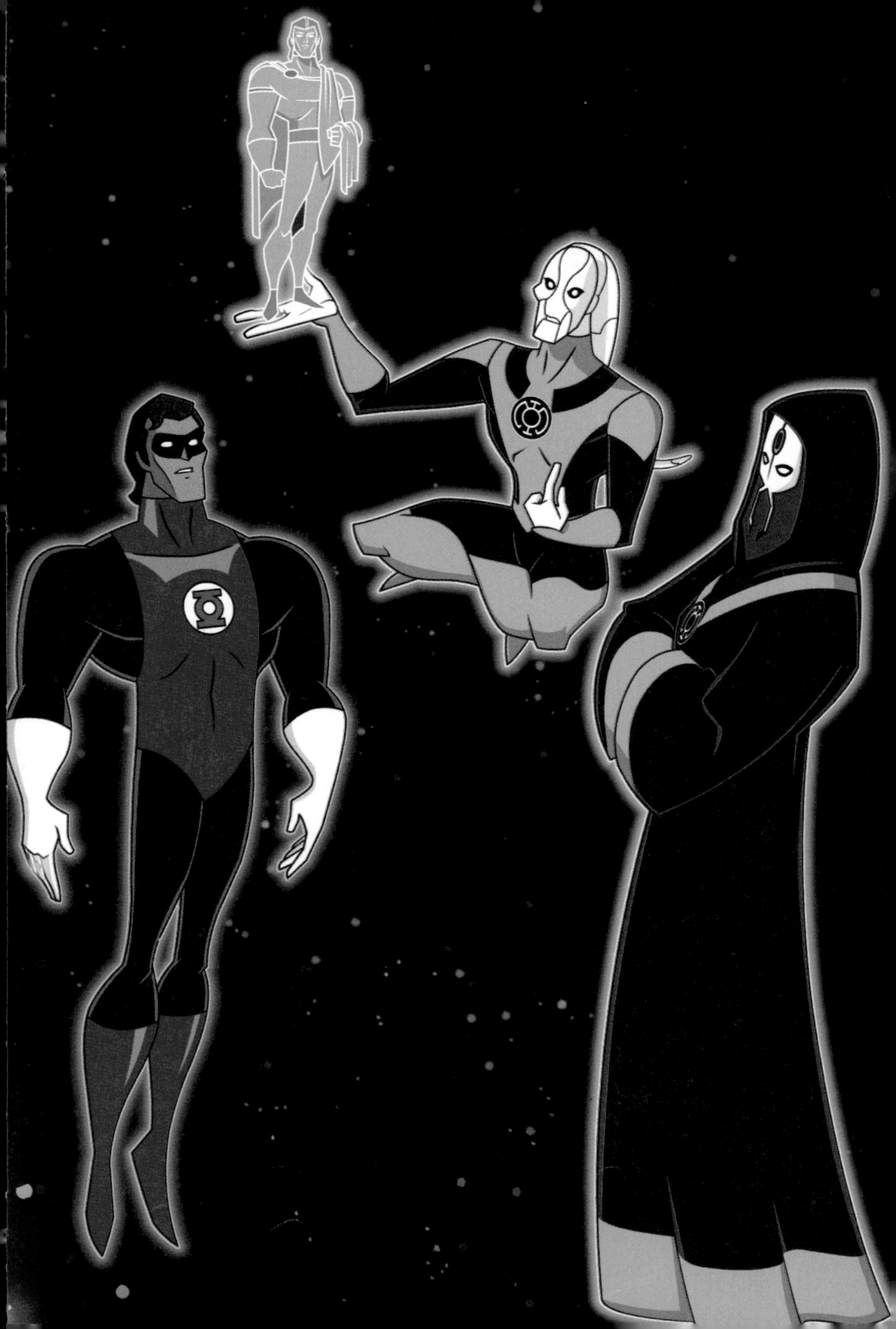

BLUE LANTERN CORPS

BASE: Odym

OFFICIAL NAME: Blue Lantern Corps

LEADERS: Ganthet and Sayd

ENEMIES: Orange Lantern Corps, Red Lantern Corps, Sinestro Corps

POWERS/ABILITIES: Unmatched hope for the future; ability to aid other corps by enhancing the Power Rings of their comrades.

BIOGRAPHY

Although exiled for their individuality, former Guardians of the Universe, Ganthet and Sayd, had great hope for the future. With this emotion, they created Blue Power Rings and founded the Blue Lantern Corps. Members of this group, including Saint Walker and Brother Sepdifer, use their rings to aid other Lantern Corps. Although extremely powerful, Blue power rings must be near a Green Lantern ring to function properly.

The Blue Lantern Corps is based on Odym. This lush, green planet is located in the Milky Way Galaxy, in space Sector 2628.

The leader of the Blue Lantern Corps chose "Saint" Bro'Dee Walker from space Sector 0001 as their first member.

Each Lantern color is powered by an emotion: Green Lanterns are fueled by willpower; Red Lanterns feed off anger; Orange Lanterns thrive on greed. Blue Lanterns get their energy from hope, the most powerful emotion in the universe.

The Blue Lantern oath:
"In fearful day, in raging night, with strong hearts full, our souls ignite! When all seems lost in the War of Light, look to the stars, for hope burns bright!"

BIOGRAPHIES

Michael Acampora was born in the Bronx, New York. He has edited various books and magazines for DC Comics and is currently pursuing degrees in Literary Arts and Political Science at Brown University. He splits his time living with his family in Somers, New York, and friends in Providence, Rhode Island. This is his first children's book.

Dan Schoening was born in Victoria, B.C., Canada. From an early age, Dan has had a passion for animation and comic books. Currently, Dan does freelance work in the animation and game industry and spends a lot of time with his lovely little daughter, Paige.

GLOSSARY

android (AN-droid)—a robot that looks and acts like a human being

cockpit (KOK-pit)—the section in the front of a plane where the pilot sits

colonize (KOL-uh-nize)—to establish a new colony, or place where people settle and live

comrade (KOM-rad)—a companion in combat

construct (KON-struhkt)—something built or made by the power of the mind

corps (KOR)—a group of people acting together

guardian (GAR-dee-uhn)—someone who guards or protects something

hologram (HOL-uh-gram)—an image made by light that looks three-dimensional

orb (ORB)—an object in space that is shaped like a sphere or a ball

regal (REE-guhl)—fit for a king or queen

willpower (WIL-pou-ur)—the ability to control what you will and will not do

DISCUSSION QUESTIONS

1. The Blue Lanterns and Hal Jordan relied on each other for help. Have you ever relied on someone? How did that person help you?

2. Each Lantern color is powered by an emotion. What emotion best describes you? Is your emotion a strength or a weakness? Explain.

3. Do you think Hal Jordan will become the greatest Green Lantern of all? Why or why not?

WRITING PROMPTS

1. Everyone has a few favorite super heroes! Who are yours? Make a list of your top ten super heroes. Does Hal Jordan make your list?

2. If you could travel to any planet in the solar system, where would you go? Write about where you would travel and why.

3. The Green Lantern ring can create anything the wearer imagines. If you had a ring, what would you imagine it to create? Write about your creation, and then draw a picture of it.

MORE NEW GREEN LANTERN ADVENTURES!

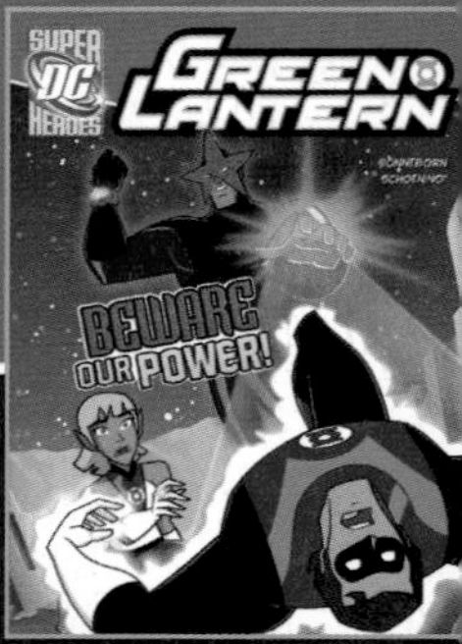
SUPER DC HEROES
GREEN LANTERN
BEWARE OUR POWER!

BEWARE OUR POWER!

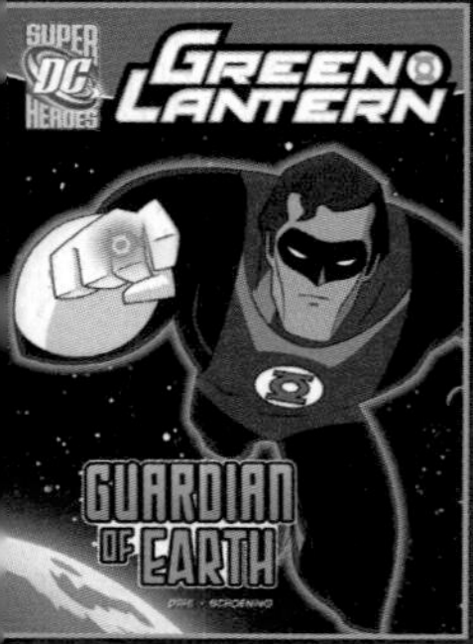
SUPER DC HEROES
GREEN LANTERN
GUARDIAN OF EARTH

GUARDIAN OF EARTH

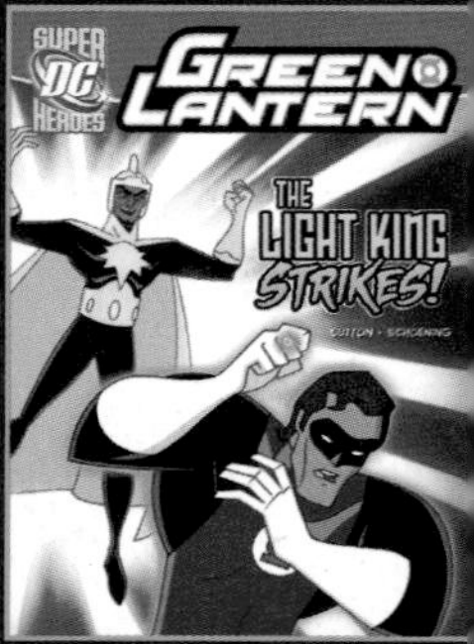
SUPER DC HEROES
GREEN LANTERN
THE LIGHT KING STRIKES!

THE LIGHT KING STRIKES!

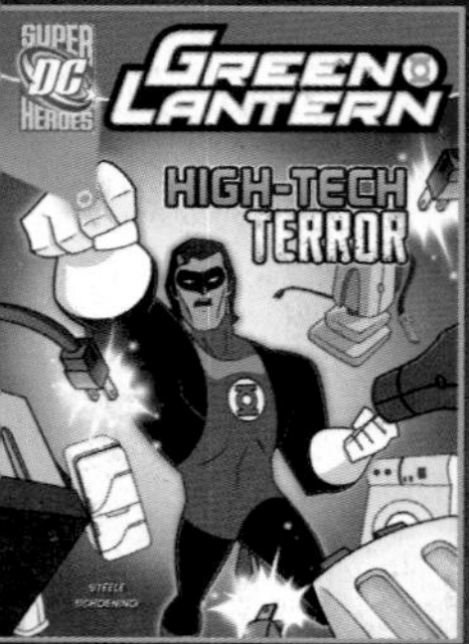
SUPER DC HEROES
GREEN LANTERN
HIGH-TECH TERROR

HIGH-TECH TERROR

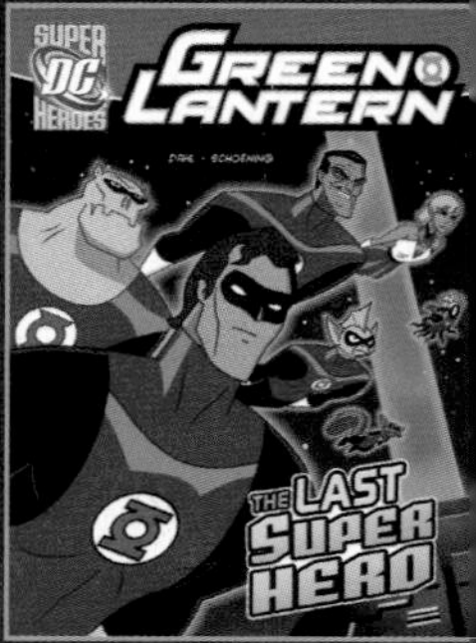
SUPER DC HEROES
GREEN LANTERN
THE LAST SUPER HERO

THE LAST SUPER HERO

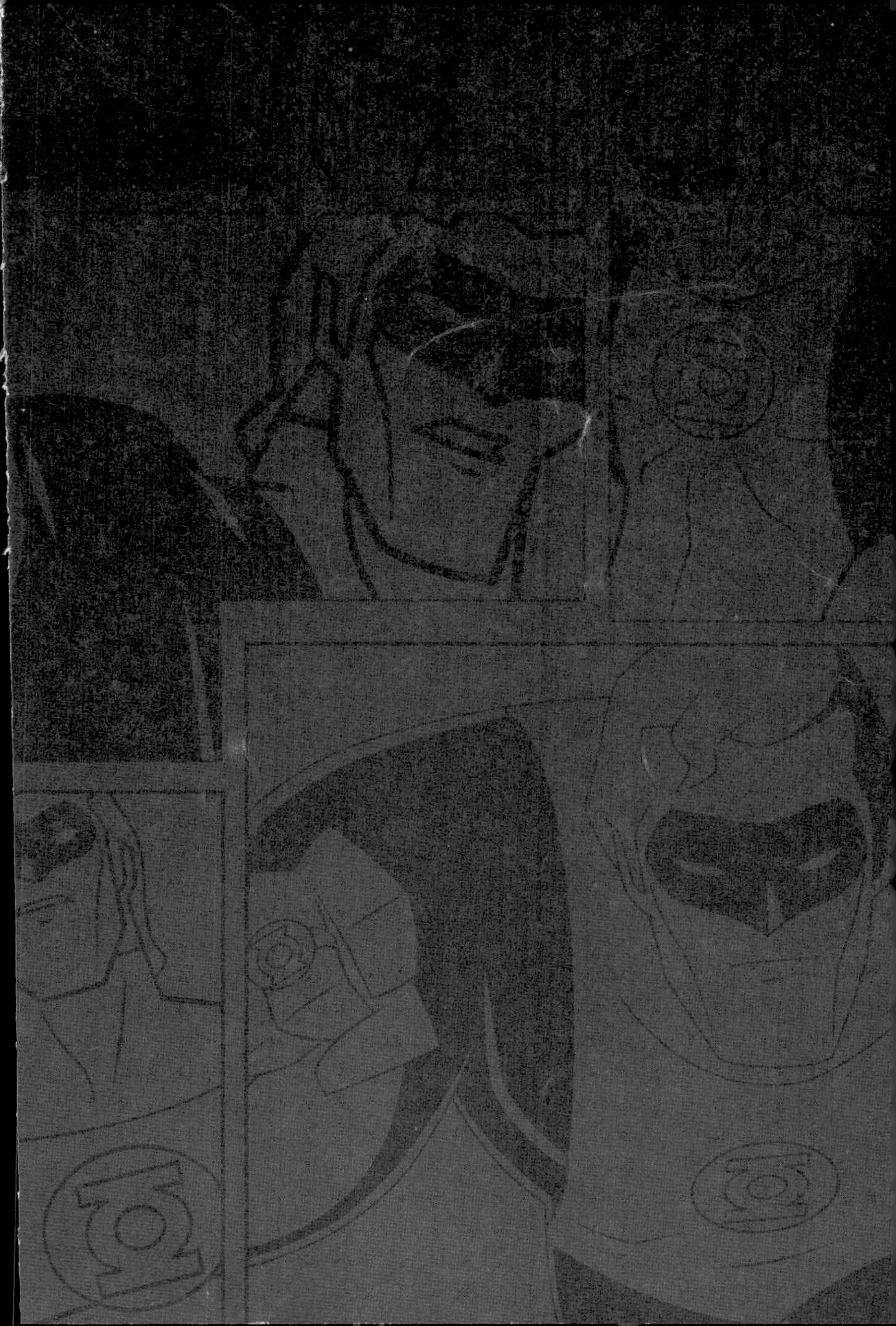

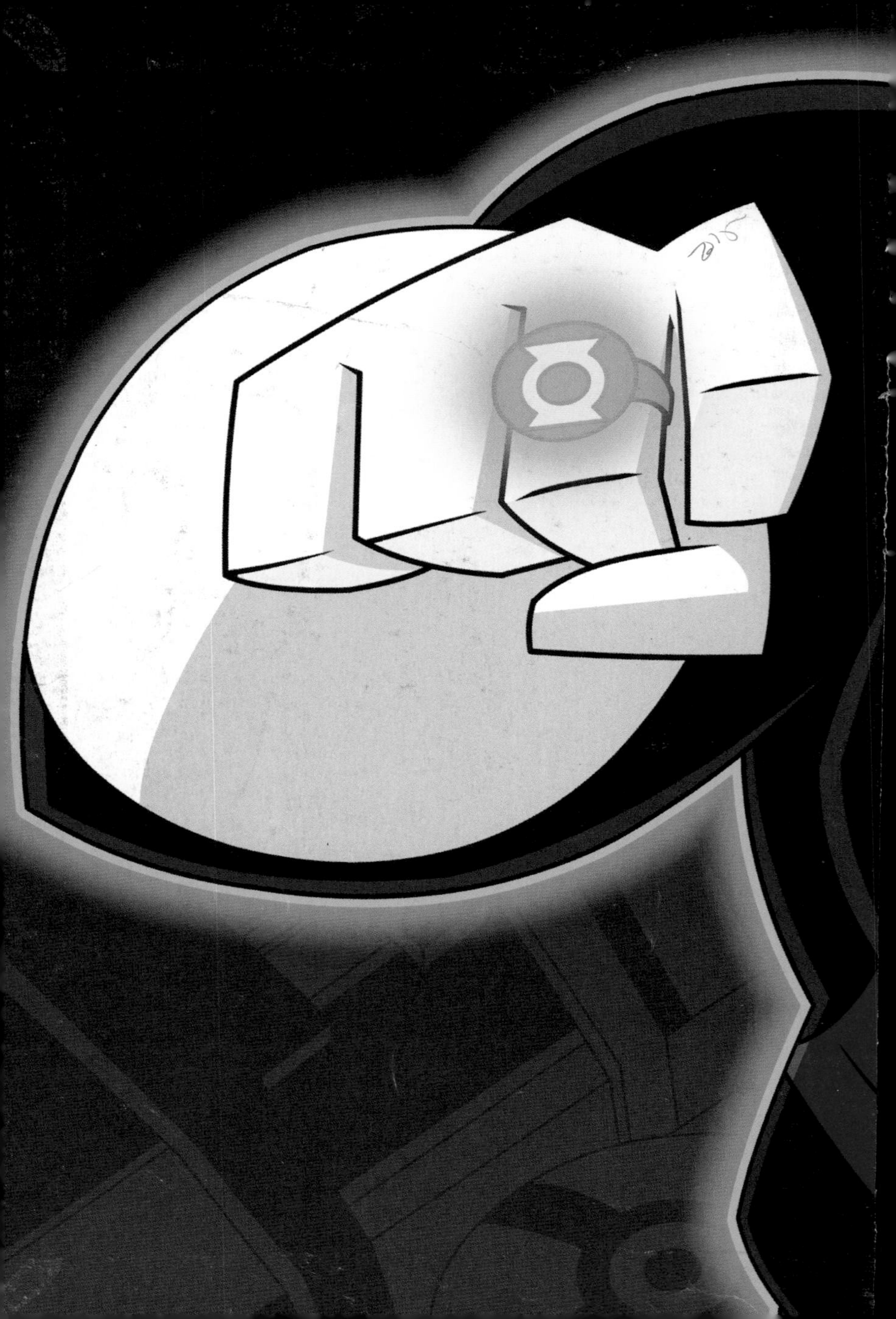